Delta Public Library

BR
BAC

D1468740

JUN 1 8 2015

Rescue Patrol

adapted by Catherine Lukas
based on the original teleplay
by McPaul Smith
illustrated by The Artifact Group

Ready-to-Read

SIMON SPOTLIGHT/NICK JR.
New York   London   Toronto   Sydney

Based on the TV series *Nick Jr. The Backyardigans*™ as seen on Nick Jr.®

SIMON SPOTLIGHT
An imprint of Simon & Schuster Children's Publishing Division
1230 Avenue of the Americas, New York, New York 10020
© 2006 Viacom International Inc. All rights reserved.
NICK JR., *Nick Jr. The Backyardigans*, and all related titles, logos, and characters are trademarks
of Viacom International Inc. NELVANA™ Nelvana Limited. CORUS™ Corus Entertainment Inc.
All rights reserved, including the right of reproduction in whole or in part in any form.
SIMON SPOTLIGHT, READY-TO-READ, and colophon are registered trademarks of Simon & Schuster, Inc.
Manufactured in the United States of America
First Edition
2 4 6 8 10 9 7 5 3 1

Cataloging-in-Publication Data for this book is available from the Library of Congress.
ISBN-13: 978-1-4169-1796-0
ISBN-10: 1-4169-1796-9

"We are Mounties on duty!

We have a big job," says .

TYRONE

"We guard a snow ,"

FORT

says  .

PABLO

"Inside the  is a big ⬤ ,"
FORT   SNOWBALL

says 🦛 .
TYRONE

"Yes," says  PABLO .

"We must guard our SNOWBALL

from SNOWBALL burglars."

"We are  patrollers!

SKI

We have a big job!"

says  .

UNIQUA

"Yes," says  TASHA .

"We rescue people

who are stuck

in the SNOW."

"Yum! That hot

COCOA

smells good," says 🐛 .

UNIQUA

"We save the  COCOA

for the people

we rescue!" says TASHA .

" , do you see any

PABLO

SNOWBALL

burglars?" asks .

TYRONE

"Not yet," says .

PABLO

"Do you see anyone

who needs help in the  ?"

SNOW

asks  .

TASHA

"Not yet," says _{UNIQUA}.

"Look! Someone is coming!"

says .

TYRONE

"Help me close the  !"

DOOR

"I heard a call for help!"

says .

TASHA

"It came from that  !"

FORT

"  patrollers to the rescue!"

SKI

says .

UNIQUA

"To the roof!" says  .

TYRONE

"We can see better

from up there!"

"We can climb this  ."

LADDER

The  slips on the ice .

LADDER

PABLO and TYRONE

land in the soft SNOW.

TASHA and UNIQUA

pull PABLO and TYRONE

out of the SNOW.

"We saved you!" says TASHA.

"Thanks," says .
PABLO

"We must have scared

away the ⬤ burglars,"
SNOWBALL

says 🦌.
TYRONE

"We Mounties did our job!"

says .

TYRONE

"We  patrollers did our job!"

says SKI TASHA.

"Who wants a snack?"

asks  .

UNIQUA

"We have hot !"

COCOA